Kai-lan's Beach Day

Alameda Free Library
1550 Oak Street

adapted by Maggie Testa

based on the screenplay written by Susan Kim

illustrated by Dave Walston

Ready-to-Read

Simon Spotlight/Nickelodeon
New York   London   Toronto   Sydney

Based on the TV series *Ni Hao, Kai-lan!*™ as seen on Nick Jr.®

SIMON SPOTLIGHT
An imprint of Simon & Schuster Children's Publishing Division
1230 Avenue of the Americas, New York, New York 10020
© 2010 Viacom International Inc. All rights reserved. NICKELODEON, *Ni Hao, Kai-lan!*,
and all related titles, logos, and characters are trademarks of Viacom International Inc.
All rights reserved, including the right of reproduction in whole or in part in any form.
SIMON SPOTLIGHT, READY-TO-READ, and colophon are registered
trademarks of Simon & Schuster, Inc.
For information about special discounts for bulk purchases, please contact
Simon & Schuster Special Sales at 1-866-506-1949 or business@simonandschuster.com.
Manufactured in the United States of America 0710 LAK
2 4 6 8 10 9 7 5 3
Library of Congress Cataloging-in-Publication Data
Testa, Maggie.
Kai-lan's beach day / adapted by Maggie Testa ; based on the teleplay written by Susan Kim.
—1st ed.
p. cm. — (Ready-to-read)
"Based on the TV series Ni Hao, Kai-lan as seen on Nickelodeon"—Copyright p.
ISBN 978-1-4424-0179-2
I. Kim, Susan, 1958- II. Ni Hao Kai-lan (Television program) III. Title.
PZ7.T2876Kai 2010
[E]—dc22
2009025270

Ni hao! I'm 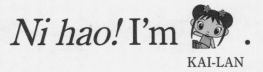.

KAI-LAN

Today is beach day!

My friends and I are

going to the beach.

Would you like to come too?

Super! Let's go, go, go!

At the beach
I like to find SEASHELLS

and dig in the SAND

with my SHOVEL.

 likes

YEYE

to fly his 🦉.

KITE

Flying his 🦉

KITE

makes 👴 feel calm.

YEYE

"Look what I found,"

says .
HOHO

Do you see what  found?
HOHO

Right, little !
CRABS

The  are digging
CRABS

in the .
SAND

They find some
SEASHELLS

and give them to us. That is

so nice!

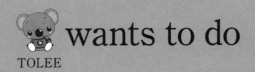 wants to do

TOLEE

something nice for the .

CRABS

"I know!" says 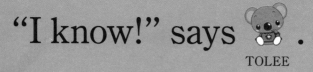 .
TOLEE

"We should build the
CRABS

a big  ."
SAND CASTLE

What a super idea!

"Let's make the

SAND CASTLE

over here," says .

TOLEE

"The is very smooth."

SAND

 wants the

TOLEE   SAND CASTLE

to be just right.

We are helping TOLEE

build the . SAND CASTLE

We are digging up SAND

and putting it into our . BUCKETS

Look,  is

TOLEE

building a big .

TOWER

The  are going

CRABS

to love their new .

SAND CASTLE

"Oh, no!" cries .

A big knocks

down the .
TOWER

"I have to start all over,"

says .
TOLEE

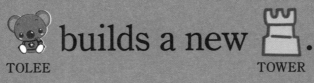 builds a new .

TOLEE   TOWER

"Oh, no!" he cries.

A big knocks

WAVE

down the again.

TOWER

"Go away, waves!"

says .

TOLEE

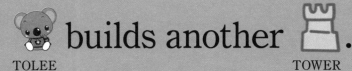 builds another .

TOLEE   TOWER

"Oh, no!" he cries.

Another big

WAVE

knocks the  down

TOWER

for the third time.

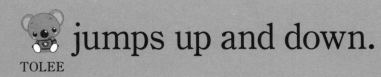 jumps up and down.

TOLEE

He stomps his

FEET

all over the 🏰 .

SAND CASTLE

We gotta, gotta try to find the reason why 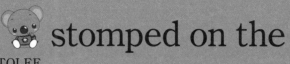 stomped on the .

TOLEE

SAND CASTLE

Do you know why?

Right!

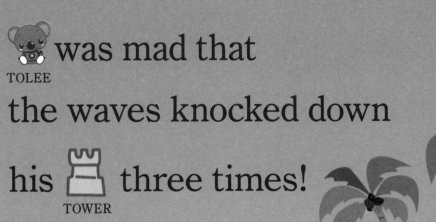 was mad that

the waves knocked down

his  three times!

says he does not

want to build another .

But we promised the

we'd make one for them.

Oh, no! What can we do?

Let's ask .

He can help us!

"We need to show
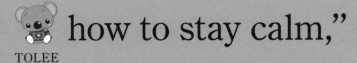 how to stay calm,"
TOLEE

says .
YEYE

 stays calm by
YEYE

swaying from side to side,

just like a !
KITE

Let's go help  calm down.
TOLEE

Look!  is swaying with us.
TOLEE

"I don't feel mad anymore," he says.

"I feel really, really calm. I'm sorry I stomped on the ."

SAND CASTLE

"Let's build a new  !"

SAND CASTLE

says 🐨.

TOLEE

Yay!

The  love their  .

CRABS

SAND CASTLE

"Thank you, ,"

TOLEE

they say.

I'm so glad you came

to the beach with us.

You make my ♥ feel super

HEART

happy.